D1345236

91120000241306

Pirate Treasure

By Christophe Miraucourt
Illustrated by Delphine Vaufrey

W
FRANKLIN WATTS
LONDON • SYDNEY

Meet the Crew

Ricky

Melinda

Mrs Seafoam

Fatbeak

Captain Sproggobbler

Captain Crook

CHAPTER 1
Sproggobbler's Teddy Bear

While their pirate dad, Gingerbeard, was off seeking treasure, Ricky and Melinda were staying with Mrs Seafoam at the *Shipwrecked Sailor's Tavern* in Shinbone's Cove.

As Ricky and Melinda were fighting over a teddy bear, Ricky nearly skidded into a grumpy pirate.

"Great Galleons of Gold-Red Garnets!" he roared. "Watch out, boy!"

"Just you wait for your dad to get back, you two!" Mrs Seafoam yelled at them while she was cooking her famous squid stew.

"I'm sure squid is cleverer than you," Melinda shouted at her brother, tugging at one of the teddy bear's paws.

"Well you're slower than a tortoise!" Ricky shouted, pulling at another paw.

"Trouble ahead!"

Fatbeak the

parrot squawked...

...but it was too late: RIP!

The teddy was torn in two!

Disaster! Ricky and Melinda had destroyed Captain Sproggobbler's teddy bear. He was the most terrifying pirate of the Caribbean! Although he had been missing for the last ten years, the mention of his name still made people shiver.

"It's your fault Ricky!" Melinda decided.

"If you hadn't pulled it so hard, it wouldn't have happened!" Ricky shouted back.

Fatbeak noticed something shiny on the floor and flew down to pick it up.

"What's that?" Ricky asked.

"It's a pendant. It must have been hidden in the teddy," Melinda muttered.

While Melinda examined the pendant, a pirate with a golden earring watched them from the bar.

"Do you think it belongs to Sproggobbler?" Ricky asked.

"Probably," Melinda said. "It's funny, it looks a bit like a bone," she added, placing it around her neck.

They didn't notice the pirate with the golden earring leaving the tavern, rubbing his hands together.

CHAPTER 2
Kidnapped!

Night was fast approaching. After her last customers had left, Mrs Seafoam sewed the teddy back together.

All of a sudden there was a loud bang! The door of the tavern swung open and a group of scary pirates rushed in.

"Run for your life!" squawked Fatbeak, escaping through the window. In a flash, Mrs Seafoam was locked in the basement and Ricky and Melinda had been kidnapped!

"Leave me alone!" Ricky cried as he tried to struggle free. Melinda recognised the golden earring on the pirate leader and gasped: "You were in the tavern this afternoon!"

The pirate took a few threatening steps towards her. Melinda could feel her heart pounding as she spoke: "I am Melinda the Terrible, daughter of Gingerbeard, granddaughter of Blackbeard, and great-granddaughter of Redbeard. Free us at once or you'll hear from my dad."

"I am Christopher Crook, captain of the *Shark*. This pendant now belongs to me!" he said, snatching it from Melinda's neck.

"Give it back! It's mine!" Melinda yelled.

"Never!" Christopher Crook sneered at her. "Now I know where Sproggobbler has hidden his treasure!" he laughed.

Then the pirate grabbed the teddy bear and searched frantically for something inside it. “This pendant should come with a map! Where is it?” he growled. “There was a map in the teddy, but I’ve burnt it,” Melinda lied. The pirate went red with rage. “But I’ve memorised most of it,” Melinda quickly added. She glanced at her brother, hoping he had understood her trick. “And I’ve memorised the rest of it!” he claimed.

“Then you shall take me to the treasure,” the pirate bellowed. “And if you lied, I’ll feed you to the sharks.” Then he turned round and shouted: “Mr Croc! Take care of our prisoners!” Mr Croc had a chain of sharp crocodile teeth around his neck, which explained his nickname. He tied up Melinda and Ricky.

As they hopped aboard the *Shark*, Melinda saw Mrs Seafoam in the distance. But it was too late: the boat was already on the move.

Once at sea, Mr Croc untied the children and locked them in the hold.

"Christopher Crook seems very determined," Ricky said.

"Don't worry," his sister answered.

"As soon as we reach land, we'll escape."

"I knew you had a plan!" he smiled.

Since there was nothing else to do, they decided to lie down on the straw mattress.

"It smells like rotten fish," Ricky moaned.

Melinda thought it smelled like Ricky's bedroom, but decided it was not the right time to start a fight. Lulled by the rocking of the ship, they fell fast asleep.

CHAPTER 3
Journey to Skeleton Island

The next day, Ricky and Melinda were allowed out on the deck of the *Shark*. Fatbeak, who had followed them, suddenly shrieked: “Beware of the pirates!”

“Fatbeak, I’m so glad you’re here!” Melinda sighed in relief.

From the front of the boat, Melinda and Ricky could see a bone-shaped island in the distance.

"Look at that!" Ricky cried out. "It's the same shape as the pendant!"

"So that's how Christopher Crook knew where to sail," Melinda whispered.

She turned to Mr Croc: "What's the island called?" she asked.

"Aye, it's Skeleton Island," he trembled.

"Drop the anchor and ready the row boat!" ordered Captain Crook. He pointed at the dinghy with the tip of his sword.

"All aboard, me hearties!"

They landed on a beach next to a shipwreck and Fatbeak followed.

As it was getting dark, Christopher Crook set up camp and Mr Croc lit a fire. The pirates decided to celebrate their soon-to be-found treasure with lots of rum.

"Perfect," whispered Melinda. "Let's rest while they're having fun."

She woke up a few hours later. It was still night and the pirates were now all fast asleep. “Time to go!” she whispered.

She wrapped a scarf around her head and collected the pirates’ swords. Ricky crept quietly towards Christopher Crook. He was sleeping like a baby, clutching his hat tightly in his hands. Ricky knew what was hidden under that hat.

He quickly grabbed the teddy bear and the pendant and put Crook’s hat on his head.

Meanwhile, Melinda was lighting a torch. “Let’s take the path that goes up this cliff,” she decided. “From there, we should be able to see if there are any people on the island.”

They followed the path, which turned into a very narrow ledge. With each step, rocks fell from beneath their feet, deep into the sea. It was a very dangerous mission!

A dark shadow soon hovered over them.

“Fatbeak!” they cried out.

“Straight ahead, me hearties!” he ordered, landing on Melinda’s shoulder.

Soon, they came across a tunnel leading into the cliff. Inside, it was as pitch-black as a cannon barrel.

"I'm not going in there," Ricky whimpered.

Melinda pointed at her brother's hat.

"A true pirate never runs away from danger!" she reminded him. "Let's go!"

"Let's see who runs away when we stumble upon skeletons," Ricky warned her.

Melinda and Fatbeak just carried on, so Ricky quickly followed.

CHAPTER 4
A Lucky Escape!

Melinda and Ricky were quite far into the tunnel when Melinda suddenly stopped.

"What's wrong?" Ricky asked.

Melinda gasped. In the darkness it seemed as if the walls were glowing.

With the tip of her sword, she scratched the surface and a shiny powder fell on the blade, making it glow instantly. After a few more steps, they were out in the open, and the sun was rising. All around them were mountains with skulls and skeletons carved into them.

"I'm not going any further," whimpered Ricky, nervously.

"Retreat!" Fatbeak screeched.

"Don't be such wimps," Melinda scolded them. She wasn't feeling any braver but she lifted her sword and shouted: "I am Melinda the Terrible, daughter of Gingerbeard, granddaughter of Blackbeard and great-granddaughter of Redbeard.

I will not be scared of skeletons!"

They continued along a path through the mountains until they were forced to stop. A chest lay in the middle of the path in front of them. "Sproggobbler's treasure!" Ricky cheered as he rushed towards it.

"Wait! Don't open it!" Melinda shouted.
But it was too late...

It was a trap which triggered rocks to fall from the mountain above. Melinda pushed Ricky out of the way just in time. A massive rock now lay where he had stood only a second ago.

"Phew! That was close," Ricky said.

A while later, they reached a village in the middle of a valley.

"Do you think people live here?" Ricky asked.

Suddenly a crowd of farmers with forks and scythes gathered around them.

"We're in trouble!" said Ricky, shuddering.

One of the farmers moved forward, shouting: "You are on forbidden land. Follow me!"

CHAPTER 5
Sproggobbler's Secret

The farmer brought Ricky and Melinda through the village to a barn. Inside, a tall, dark shadow towered in front of them. With the full-grown fuzzy beard, the scruffy hair and deep dark eyes, surely it had to be...

"Captain Sproggobbler!" Ricky, Melinda and Fatbeak all cried at once.

"Rumbling Roasted Red Radishes!" the captain said. "I'm not deaf, no need to shout!" Two children the same age as Ricky and Melinda stepped out of the barn.

"What's up, Granddad?" they asked.

Melinda and Ricky looked at each in surprise. Not only was Sproggobbler alive but he was also a granddad!

“Who are you?” Sproggobbler boomed.

“And what are you doing here?”

“I am Melinda, daughter of Gingerbeard!”

“And I am Ricky, son of Gingerbeard!”

“Are you really Gingerbeard’s children?”

Sproggobbler replied.

“A most brave pirate!

We’ve shared many

a barrel of rum

together!”

Ricky and Melinda had no idea that their father knew the captain! Melinda handed him the teddy and the pendant.

"Here, these are yours."

Now it was Sproggobbler's turn to look stunned. "My teddy and my lucky charm!" he cried. "How did you get them?"

"It's a long story." Melinda said.

"We were kidnapped by Christopher Crook," Ricky explained. "We escaped and I stole his hat."

"Blistering Booming Barley Barrels! That scoundrel again!" Sproggobbler shouted. "He was in my crew. I fired him when I discovered his plot to steal my gold!"

Then, it was Sproggobbler's turn to tell his story: "I swore that I'd wear this pendant for as long as I was a pirate. But I grew tired of being a pirate. I wanted to watch my grandchildren, Pedro and Lisa, grow up."

"So you faked your disappearance so that no one would look for you," Melinda said. "And you had to get rid of the pendant," Ricky added.

"These farmers took me in," Sproggobbler explained. "And I shared my gold to ensure we had all we needed."

"Were you the one who named the island?" Melinda asked. Sproggobbler smiled.

"It was the best way to keep curious people away. But that rascal managed to find me!"

Melinda thought fast.

"I have an idea!" she cried. "Christopher Crook and his men will have the biggest scare of their lives!"

It was nearly nightfall. Hidden behind skeleton-shaped rocks, Melinda, Ricky, Pedro and Lisa were waiting for Christopher Crook and his men.

"Won't they ever come?" Ricky whined.

"Maybe they went back?" Pedro murmured.

Soon the light from the torches of Christopher Crook's men came into view.

"Did you know that walking among skeletons is bad luck?" Mr Croc said, examining the rocks with his torch.

"That's true," all the pirates agreed.

"Let's go back."

"No way!" said Crook. "We can't let these hat thieves escape. Only they know where the treasure is. Keep following me!"

This was the moment Melinda had been waiting for! She ran out, followed by her brother and the villagers. Pedro, Lisa, Ricky and Melinda had spent the afternoon scraping the glowing powder off the walls of the cave. They used it to make a glow-in-the-dark paint. They had drawn bones on eveyone to look like scary skeletons.

In torchlight, the effect was very frightening indeed. Even Fatbeak was swooping and squawking spookily. But the most terrifying of all was Sproggobbler, whose face was glowing bright in the night. Christopher Crook and his men were shivering as if it were minus 20 degrees.

"P...p-p-please, have mercy!" Christopher Crook begged. "I am too young to die!"

Then he was out of sight, running away with his men right behind him.

All of the villagers burst out with laughter.

"That was an enlightened idea!" chuckled Pedro, pleased with the pun.

"We won't see them any time soon." Lisa predicted.

The next day, Sproggobbler sat by the campfire and told everyone his most daring tales.

But where was Fatbeak? He suddenly appeared, squawking: "It's the *Intrepid*!" Gingerbeard's ship! Fatbeak had been travelling back to alert their father!

"Well done, Fatbeak!" Melinda told him.

It was time to say goodbye.

Sproggobbler gave Ricky his teddy bear and Melinda his pendant to thank them for their help.

"We shall keep your secret!" Melinda promised him.

"Aye, I'll count on you, me hearties! You will always be welcome on Skeleton Island," he told them.

Soon the *Intrepid* came into view and anchored near the beach.

"What are we going to tell Dad?" Ricky wondered.

"We'll just explain how Christopher Crook saw Sproggobbler's ghost. After all, it's the truth!"

"The whole truth," Ricky agreed with a grin.

"Nothing but the truth!" Fatbeak squawked above them all.

MIX
Paper from
responsible sources
FSC® C104740

Franklin Watts
First published in Great Britain in 2015 by
The Watts Publishing Group

First published in French as
Le Trésor De La Pirate

English text and adaptation by Fabrice
Blanchefort.

Series Editor: Melanie Palmer
Series Advisor: Catherine Glavina
Cover Designer: Cathryn Gilbert
Design Manager: Peter Scoulding

A CIP catalogue record for this book is
available from the British Library.

ISBN 978 1 4451 3715 5 (hbk)
ISBN 978 1 4451 3717 9 (pbk)
ISBN 978 1 4451 3714 8 (ebook)
ISBN 978 1 4451 3716 2 (library ebook)

Printed in China

Franklin Watts
An imprint of
Hachette Children's Group
Part of The Watts Publishing Group
Carmelite House
50 Victoria Embankment
London EC4Y 0DZ

An Hachette UK Company
www.hachette.co.uk

www.franklinwatts.co.uk